HOW TO CATCH A
DRAGON

For Vic, Finn, Zed and Kyle, with love – CH
For Theodore xx – EE

SIMON AND SCHUSTER
First published in Great Britain in 2014
by Simon and Schuster UK Ltd
1st Floor, 222 Gray's Inn Road, London WC1X 8HB
A CBS Company

A CIP catalogue record for this book is available from the
British Library upon request

ISBN: 978-0-85707-959-6
eBook ISBN: 978-0-85707-960-2

Printed in China
10 9 8 7 6 5 4 3 2 1

HOW TO CATCH A
DRAGON

CARYL HART & ED EAVES

SIMON AND SCHUSTER
London   New York   Sydney   Toronto   New Delhi

It's just not fair.
I've been at school all week, and now I have
to do homework! How am I meant to draw
a dragon if I've never even seen one?

I'm just looking for clues in *The Trolls and Goblins Handbook* when . . .

"Albie!"

It's Mum.
"We need to pop to the library," she says. "Come on."

"But what about my **dragon drawing?**" I cry.

"You can bring it with you," she smiles.

I want to go on bikes, but Mum's books are **too heavy** so we climb into the car.

The library is HUMUNGOUS.
It looks just like a CASTLE!

AWESOME!

There are gazillions of books!

I see one called *The Dragon Spotter's Guide*. But someone else grabs it first. **Drat!**

It's a knight, dressed in REAL armour!
WOAH!

"Are you going dragon hunting?" I ask.

"I want to," says the knight. "But my brothers say I'm too small, so I'm just reading about them instead."

"Well, two small knights are easily as good as one big one," I say. "Let's go together!"

We race across the drawbridge, through the fields and out towards the Forgotten Forest.

YIPPEE!

"I'm Albie," I shout.
"I'm Sir Cuthbert Clinkety-Clank," grins t[...]

Inside the woods, it's dark and creepy.
Strange animals rustle in the leaves.
OOOOOH!
Suddenly . . .

GRRRRRRRRAAAAAAAH!

A huge grizzly bear blocks our path.

Uh-oh!

"Heellp!" I cry. "We're going to be eaten alive!"

"Don't worry," smiles Sir Clinkety-Clank.
"I know exactly what to do."

He tiptoes towards the bear and
tickles him under the chin!
"You just wanted a cuddle, didn't you?"
he says.

PHEW!

Soon we reach a grassy hillside.
"Let's have a sandwich," says Sir Clinkety-Clank.
Suddenly, the ground starts to shake.
Thud! Thud! THUD!
"Earthquake!" we yell.

But it's not an earthquake . . .

It's a hideous hairy troll! She lunges for Sir Cuthbert.
"Ooh, lovely!" she grins. "A tasty treat in a tin!"
"Oh, I wouldn't eat him if I were you," I say, bravely.

"He tastes of boiled cabbage and toenails."
The troll is disappointed.
"Never mind," I smile. "If you help us find
some dragons, you can share our picnic."

"A pickernicker?" gasps the troll. "With hegg
sanniches and pickledy bunions? Yes PLEASE!"

The troll leads us to a terrifying tunnel in the hillside.
"There's extra special draggins through 'ere!" she grins.
"Foller me."
It looks **scary.**

Ghostly wails echo from the darkness.
"W-what's that noise?" I gulp.
Sir Cuthbert grabs a lantern
and draws his sword.

"Only one way to find out," he says.

We tiptoe into the gloom.
The wailing gets louder. Suddenly a dark shape
rears up in front of us. It's moaning and
waving its tentacles!

"Heeeelp!" I cry.
But Sir Cuthbert is not scared at all.

"That's not a monster," he laughs. "It's my big brothers!"
The other knights cling to Sir Cuthbert.

"We got chased by a horrible bear and saw a hideous
troll and we've been hiding here for AGES!"

Proudly, we tell them about our adventure.
Then the troll leads us through the tunnel
and out into the sunshine.

And that's when we see them.

DRAGONS!

The valley below us is teeming with hundreds of magnificent, beautiful dragons! AWESOME!

The big knights draw their swords.
"Stop!" growls the troll. "Them draggins is friendly."
I pull my homework out of my pocket. "We don't
have to fight them," I say. "Let's draw them!"

I share out my paper and pencils and we settle down. The biggest knight sighs happily. "Drawing dragons is so much easier than catching them," he smiles.

At last the sun goes down, and the air begins to chill. So we pack up our things and head for home.

Back at the library, Mum is busy chatting.
"Sorry, Albie," she says. "I hope you haven't
been bored."
I smile at my new friends. "Nobody could
EVER be bored in a library," I say.

"Come on then," grins Mum. "I just need to
nip to the car wash and then we can go home."

Uh-oh!